SUBMIT

WHISKEY RUN HEROES

HOPE FORD

Submit © 2021 by Hope Ford

Editor: Kasi Alexander

Cover Design: Cormar Covers

1
SAMANTHA

As I pull up to the gates of the Whiskey Run office, I have my badge out in my hand ready to show the guard. But he recognizes me, waves, and opens the gates for me to drive on in.

I pull into my parking spot and notice that everyone else is already here. Nash, Knox, Walker, Brooklyn—all their trucks and SUVs are here. Well, everyone except for Bear. I don't see his truck, and I sort of kick myself for even looking for it. He was on a mission and probably got back late—heck, he may be taking the day off, for all I know.

I take a deep breath and start to think about my life in Whiskey Run. The whole team has been super nice, and this has really been a good change of pace for me. It's different than when I was stationed in Texas and was traveling nonstop and not knowing where or when I would be home again. When Walker approached me about this opportunity, I knew I had to take it. I'm 32 years old now, and more than anything, I want to settle down.

I look at myself in the rearview mirror and shake my head. Just thinking of settling down has my thoughts going to Bear, and that's the last person that I should be thinking about. The last few days have been pretty relaxing with him out of town. He's the only one that I really can't make heads or tails of. He's a big guy. That would normally be intimidating to anyone. But just looking at him causes a flare in my belly, and it's not anything that I'm ready to examine yet. I mean, why am I attracted to the one man that hasn't really been welcoming to me? It doesn't make sense.

So these last few days without his grunts and growls I've been able to relax a little at my new home here, but I know that today he'll be back, and I have to prepare myself for it. I grab my purse and my tote bag out of the passenger seat, put them over my shoulder, and walk into the front door. Brooklyn, Walker's assistant, is at her seat, and she waves me over. When I first met Brooklyn, things were weird between us but only because she thought Walker and I had a relationship or something, and that couldn't be further from the truth. He's always just been a good guy that looked out for me, but that's it. When he and Brooklyn got together, it thrilled me. It sort of sucked that she had to get kidnapped for Walker to come to his senses, but at least it all worked out in the end. Plus, seeing them together gives me hope for my future. I would give anything to have a man look at me the way Walker looks at her.

"What's up, girl?" Brooklyn asks with a smile on her face.

I just laugh. "I'm good. Is the meeting still on for this morning?"

Brooklyn nods her head. "And I believe they're all in there about to get started."

"Okay, see you after," I tell her before I pick up my stride and start to walk to my office at the back of the building. I set everything down and start digging in my tote for a notepad and pencil. With my head down, I don't hear anyone come toward me until I hear a grunt, and damn, I squeeze my thighs together without even thinking about it. I've missed that grunt. I prepare myself before lifting my head.

I lift my head and come face to face with Bear. He's staring at me intensely, but there's still not a smile on his face. I try to hide my excitement of seeing him. I can't admit how much I had missed him and even worried about him while he'd been gone. Of course, I don't know why I would. If there's anyone that could handle a mission like the one he was on, it would be him. "Hey, Bear," I say. He doesn't say anything back; his eyes just continue to search my face. For a second, I wonder if he's missed me too, but that's nonsense. I don't even think he's talked to me since I came to work here. Well, unless you count grunts. I get those all the time.

He just holds his hands out. And for the first time, I notice that he has a cup from Honeybee Coffee in one hand and then a brown bag from Sugar Glaze in his other hand. Without thinking about it, I reach for the cup and the bag and hold them up. "What is this?" I ask him.

He shrugs his shoulders. "I thought you would like those. I think they're your favorite."

My eyes widen, and I open the bag and look down, and sure enough, there is an apple turnover that is still warm in the bottom of the bag. "How did you know?" I ask him as I reach into the bag, pull it out, and take a bite without even thinking. I moan as the flavors hit my tongue. My eyes close, and I savor the taste. *Damn, that's good.*

Bear grunts again, and my eyes fly open. "This was so nice of you. Thank you for this." He seems embarrassed, but I have to ask him, "Why did you bring these to me? Did you bring some for everyone?"

He shakes his head. "No. I only brought them for you."

Before I can ask him why or how his time in Florida went, he stalks out of my office. I walk to my doorway and watch him go. My eyes are glued to his backside because how could I look at anything else? He really does a pair of denims justice.

I'm staring at him, not even thinking where I'm at, and before I know it, Brooklyn is elbowing me in the side. "Girl, I see what you're doing," she says with a laugh.

I jerk my eyes from Bear back to Brooklyn, and she's eyeing the pastry in my hand. She says, "You got a little something there," and points to my lip.

I start to wipe it off. "Oh, it must be glaze," I tell her, holding up the turnover.

She rolls her eyes. "No. It's drool."

I playfully swat at her. "Brooklyn! I'm not drooling!" But I don't sound convincing.

Brooklyn chuckles. "You obviously are, but I don't think it's one-sided. I've never seen that man act that way. If he has his sights on you, you are one lucky girl."

Brooklyn is shaking her head as she walks back over to her desk. I could stand here all day and try to analyze what's going on with Bear, but I know that I'm about to be late for the meeting. I grab my pad and pencil and put it under my arm. Then I grab the cup of coffee and eat the rest of my pastry on my way down the hall. There is no way I'm going to let it go to waste.

Bear

I WALK DOWN the hallway away from Samantha. It takes everything I have not to turn around and look at her. I know we're going to the same place. She has the same meeting to go to as I do, and I'm already about to be late, but I can't go in there—not like this. Instead of turning into the conference room, I take a side door and step outside. As soon as I'm out in the clear air, I let the door shut behind me and take three deep breaths. The Whiskey Run mountains are in front of me, and it's a beautiful view. But I can't enjoy them today because all I can think about is Samantha. She's all I've thought about since she came to work here.

I thought that since I had been gone on this mission that it would give me some perspective and some space. Enough time to get away from her or to at least get her out of my head. But it wasn't, because all I can think about is her. When I woke up this morning, I left my house early just so I could get her favorite coffee and her favorite pastry. She has me all coiled up in knots, and she doesn't even realize it. I'm standing outside with my hands on my hips, trying to will down my hard cock when Knox comes out the door.

"Hey, brother, you okay?" he asks.

I don't look at him, but I nod my head. "I'm good."

I see him pointing inside. "You know the meeting's about to start, right?"

I nod again. I should probably apologize for

being an ass, but I think that the guys all are used to me by now. This is just who I am. I don't say a lot, but when I do, it means something.

Knox finally gets tired of waiting and says, "Okay, I'm going to go on in. I'll see you in there." He doesn't move, though.

Finally I turn and say, "Let's go." I follow him inside the door and into the conference room. We're all sitting at a big table with Nash at the front. He starts the meeting talking about everything that went down the last few days with John and Madison and how the FBI was happy that we had helped them shut down the Colombian cartel. Everyone is happy, but there's not a lot of time for celebration because instantly Nash starts to hand out the files. It's like this every time missions are handed out. They're in files with all of the information already prepared on what will be happening, where we need to be, and everything else we'll need to know.

The side conversations all go on around me, and I know I should be paying attention, but all I can do is sit and stare at Samantha. I know I need to keep my mind on the mission that is probably being handed out to me as we speak. But I can't take my eyes off of her, she's so beautiful. The most beautiful woman I've ever met.

It's only when Nash says Samantha's name that I bring myself back to the conversation at hand, and then I start to pay attention. Nash is pointing to the file in his hands. "Samantha and Logan will be posing as husband and wife."

As soon as I hear it, I act on instinct. I don't even think about what I'm doing, but I push back from the table and stand up. "Nash, I need to speak with you."

He and everyone else in the room is surprised; I know they are. I never talk in these things. Heck, I never talk unless directly spoken to, but today there's no way I'm going to be quiet. He gestures to the people at the table. "Bear, can this wait? We're in the middle of a meeting."

I tell him, "No," and I don't even give him a choice. I walk over to the door and hold it open, gesturing for him to come with me. He looks surprised, and I wait for him to refuse me, fuck even fire me, but he doesn't.

He looks around the room. "We'll be back in a minute."

He walks out the door I'm holding open and stops in the hallway. He waits for the door to shut behind us before he starts. "Bear, what is this? What is going on?"

I shake my head. "Logan is not going on the mission. I will be going on the mission with Samantha."

Nash puts his hands on his hips and looks at me with surprise on his face. "You do know that I'm the boss around here, right?"

I should back down, but I can't. There's no way I'll stay here in Whiskey Run while Sam is in Miami posing as Logan's wife. It's not going to happen. "Sir, I've never questioned you before. You give an order, I do it. But this time, I can't. I'm going on this mission."

He shoves his hand through his hair. I know I've thrown him for a loop. Hell, I wouldn't be surprised if he fired me. I don't think anyone's questioned Nash. He's someone that you just do what he says to do.

"You're going on the mission?" he asks.

He's looking me in the eye, and I know that he can see there's no doubt on my face. I will be the one that goes on this mission with Samantha.

I nod my head. "Yes, I'm the one that will be going."

Nash has the nerve to laugh. "No offense, Bear, but this mission is for a married couple."

He says it like that's going to stop me. I shrug my shoulders, acting as if that's not a big deal.

He shakes his head. "You don't understand. You will have to act like you like somebody; you have to be convincing. This is not something that we're messing around with. I can't have you down there and blow our cover because you can't pull it off."

I start to think about it and try to piece together what this mission is about. I know it's in Miami, and I'm sure it has to do with the big human trafficking ring that is taking over there. I spit the words out. "I know that this is an important mission, Nash. I know how important it is. And you also know that I have never let you down before. Let me do this."

Nash tilts his head to the side and looks at me. He crosses his arms over his chest. "Do you think that this is a good idea, Bear? Obviously there's something that you've got going on here to feel this strongly about it. Do you think that it's going to be a good idea for you and Samantha to do this together?"

I grit my teeth together, frustrated that he would even ask. "I will do my job. I will bring Samantha back home safe, and whatever this mission entails, I will do it. You do not have to question me because I will make sure the job gets done."

I stare at him, waiting and hoping that he's going to give me the answer that I want. Finally, he lets out a big breath. "Okay, I hope I'm not making a mistake here, Bear."

I let out the breath I've been holding. "I won't let you down, sir." And then I go back into the meeting before he has a chance to change his mind.

2

SAMANTHA

It's awkward. That is for sure. I can feel everyone's eyes on me as Bear and Nash walk out of the room. At first, nobody says a thing. Everyone is wide-eyed, looking at each other. I've never heard anybody interrupt Nash before. And when Bear did it, I held my breath waiting to see how he was going to respond to that. Nash seemed to take it in stride and even seemed okay with it. But now here I sit, and I know that my face is red wondering if this is all because of me. Being a woman in this field, I've had to prove myself over and over. I really didn't feel like I had to do that here. Walker vouched for me, and everyone seemed to take it in stride and accept me as one of the team. Well, everyone except for Bear with his grumpy ass. I swear if he's out there telling Nash I'm not ready for this mission, I'm going to lose it on him.

Eventually, the guys start to talk, and they mention the trip to Florida. Thankfully, the mission was a success. Everything was resolved except there were a few hiccups, like when Madison showed up at the drop when Knox was supposed to be guarding her at the hotel.

"Man, I had fun in Florida. I wouldn't mind going back. How about it, Sam? I can pose as the husband if it means I get to relax beachside."

Logan slaps Knox on the back and starts laughing. "Yeah, that's not going to happen. I bet you're on desk duty for letting Madison skip out."

Knox instantly looks at John. "I'm sorry, man. Who would have thought your girl would be an ex-gymnast and could scale the side of buildings?"

Everyone is laughing when the doors open, but instantly the whole room quiets. Every eye in the room is on Bear and Nash as they walk back in. I try to read their body language, but neither one of them seems mad. They seem normal. Well, normal for Bear, anyway. He still has a scowl on his face.

Bear takes his seat, and instead of looking at

Nash, he looks straight at me. My whole body turns hot, and I can feel myself start to sweat. There are butterflies in my stomach, and I'm so confused on how I could be mad at him only moments ago, thinking he's jeopardizing my job, and now I'm all turned on with just a look. *Pull yourself together, Sam,* I tell myself.

I have to pull my eyes from him and look at Nash. He holds his hands up and clears his throat. "There's a change in plans. It will be Bear and Samantha making the trip to Miami."

Everybody tries to act like they're not surprised, but it's obvious that everyone is caught off guard. Nash doesn't take any notice. He addresses Logan since Dylan is home with Jenna and the new baby. "I'm gonna need you to take over on tech today. I need some IDs for Bear and Samantha, and I need their histories swiped and clean. I have the profiles of what I want in the folder."

Logan nods his head and agrees.

Nash continues to go over details, and I know I should be listening, but I'm not. My thoughts are a jumbled mess on what is happening, and soon after, Nash must call the meeting over because everyone starts to get up.

It seems that they're all scurrying to the door as fast as they can. I wait until the room is clear and stop next to Bear, who's still sitting in his seat, looking over the file in his hands. "Uh, Bear, can I see you outside for a minute?"

He merely nods his head, and I follow him out the side door to the back. Any other time I come out this door, I'm always in awe of the mountains, but not today. Today I'm seething mad as I stare at Bear. "What is your problem?"

His forehead creases as if he's confused or something, and I know that he's not. He can't be. He has to realize the scene he just caused in there and what it did to me. Now everyone is going to be questioning me and my performance. I take a step toward him. "What is it? You don't think I can handle myself? You want to be there in Miami to micromanage everything I do? Do you know that I was a first sergeant in the Army? Do you know that I have fought in war on the frontlines? I can do this without you there telling me what I'm doing wrong."

I'm spitting mad by the time I'm done, and it makes it even worse when he just crosses his arms over his chest. "Are you done?" he asks me calmly.

I shake my head and throw my hands in the air.

"Forget it. I'm going to go talk to Nash. I'm not going to Miami with you, Bear."

He puts his hand on the door but doesn't open it. "You're going with me or you're not going."

I'm seething mad and so freakin' frustrated. I'm going back and forth on whether I want to smack him on the face or kiss him. Damn it. I shake my head. "Well, I won't go then," I snarl at him.

He's still holding the door closed. "There were 35 women kidnapped this month alone, just through this organization that we're going to get intel on. You're telling me that you're going to let them get away with it because you don't want to go on a trip with me?"

I rear back and look at him. It's the most he's ever said in one sentence to me. Heck, it's probably the most he's ever said to me period. "It's not that I don't want to go on a trip with you. I just—"

He interrupts me. "I'll be on that plane to Miami. If you're not, then you're not the woman I thought you were." He barely gets the words out and he jerks the door open and walks back inside.

I let it shut behind him and try to calm myself down. I don't even understand what is happening right now. How could he be so sweet this morning? Well, sweet for Bear, anyway. He brought me my favorite coffee and my favorite pastry. And now he's issuing demands and messing with my job. I don't understand any of it. But I'll be damned if he's going to control what I do here. I love living in Whiskey Run, and I'm not going to let him interfere with my job.

3
BEAR

I TRY TO HIDE MY SMIRK WHEN I SEE SAMANTHA walking down the aisle of the airplane. I had no doubt that she would come. It's in her nature, and she's not a quitter. There's no way she would bypass her responsibility. This is part of her job, and as far as I can tell, she loves this job. Plus, she's not the type that could live with it on her conscience knowing she could help other women and then not doing it.

I scoot my legs in as she moves into the seat next to me. When she sits down, it's apparent how much bigger I am than her. I try to scrunch in my shoulders and arms so as not to touch her. Touching her is not a good thing. My body reacts just being close to her; touching her would be a whole new ballgame. I inhale deeply and then wish I hadn't. She has on that soft floral scent that has my balls drawing in tight and my cock lengthening in my jeans. Fuck, let's get the plane in the air already. The sooner we get there, the sooner we can get some space between us. Not that I'm going to let her out of my sight or anything, but yeah, I at least need her out of arms' length. It's either that or I'm going to do something that will embarrass us both.

She huffs loudly as if she's letting me know she hasn't forgotten yesterday and hands me a file. Her words are very clipped, and it's obvious that she is still mad at me. "I'm here," she says.

I nod and look at her. "I'm glad you came."

She obviously expected me to say something else because her face softens, and then as if she catches herself, she instantly goes into work mode. I can't really blame her for being mad. She's tried to prove herself ever since she got to the team. And I know that I came across as an asshole by having Logan taken off the job so that I could go, but I'm not really ready to explain my reasoning yet.

I open the file and start to scan all the pertinent information of this mission. My name is Liam Smith. I'm thirty-five years old. I own a construction company. It then goes on to talk about my wife Samantha Smith. She's thirty-two. She's a stay-at-home mom to our two children. I keep reading and notice that we are on a vacation for our five-year anniversary.

I pat the pocket of my shirt and pull out the diamond ring I've had there since I boarded the plane. I hand it over to her with a gruff "here."

She holds her hand out, and I drop the box in her hand. Her eyes go from me to the box and then me again. I nod my head, gesturing for her to open it. When she does, she gasps loudly before looking around at everyone that is sitting down and getting their seatbelts on. She ducks her head, holding up the ring as if letting the light shine off of it. She whispers to me, "This is so beautiful. Where did Nash get this at? It probably set him back quite a bit." She takes it out and puts it on her finger. "Surely the jeweler will let him return it, though."

I should probably leave it alone and let her think what she thinks. But that's not in my nature. "I bought it," I say and watch her eyes widen.

To say she's surprised is putting it mildly. She tries to take it off, and I put my hand out to stop her. My hand wraps around hers easily. I ignore the spark that shoots up my arm and watch as she shakes her head.

"But..." She shakes her head, her eyes wide. "What if something happens? I can't risk losing it."

I squeeze her hand gently. "No. Please don't take it off. Nothing's going to happen."

She tilts her head and says a little louder this time, "You don't know that. Anything can happen in this line of work. You know that, and I'm not willing to risk losing your ring. Why do you even have a ring like this?" She sits back, eyes wide, and gasps. "Oh my God, am I wearing your ex-girlfriend's ring or something?"

"No," I tell her instantly. I mean, what kind of man does she think I am? As if I'd ever put another woman's ring on her finger. Fuck, at this point I can't even remember any woman before her... at least I don't want to.

I take my hand back and drop it to the file in my lap. I'm definitely not going to be getting into all of that with her. She doesn't need to know that I picked this ring up the day that I met her. Even to me, that sounds crazy. She'd probably go running off the plane if she found out. Probably even put out a restraining order, and I can't say I'd blame her.

She waves her hand in front of my face. "Bear... Earth to Bear. Are you going to explain this to me?"

I shrug my shoulders as if it doesn't matter to me at all. "It's done now, and we don't have a choice. These are the rings that we have to wear." I show her my hand with the matching wedding band.

She wants to keep arguing with me or at least get answers, but when I give her the look—the one that says I'm not going to give in—she finally shrugs in defeat. She gives up, knowing that I'm not going to give her an answer, and she shoves the ring back firmly onto her finger.

"I told Nash I'd take care of it, and I did," I tell her as if that's enough reason.

Her hands start to fidget in her lap. "Is this how this is going to be? You're going to tell me what is going to happen, and you just expect me to go along with it? I'm not made that way. That's not who I am. I'm independent and don't appreciate being told what to do, how to do it, or when to do it."

I look around at the passengers around us, and I don't take the bait. I'm not going to get into an argument with her here. I don't want to argue with her. So when she finishes, I just smirk, which probably pisses her off more. But it's either I piss her off or I kiss her. I'm willing to bet the latter wouldn't end well. "Is this our first argument as husband and wife?"

She rolls her eyes and takes a deep breath. I can tell she's trying to get herself together, which I hate because I like it when she gets all riled up.

Sam

I LEAN BACK in my seat and take three calming breaths. I've had my eyes on Bear ever since I spotted him from the front of the plane and then had to climb over him to get to my seat. Obviously, I'm taking everything to heart and being erratic, because just being this close to him is messing with all of my senses. He's a big man. I know he's a big man. But sitting next to him, this close, just makes me feel dainty and petite... and protected. A part of me hates that feeling. I've never thought about it this way, but I'm not the type of woman that wants to be protected. At least I didn't think I was. But here I am sitting next to this big, alpha man and loving how it makes me feel. Maybe I don't want just any man to be protective of me. But Bear I do. When I get myself together, I look down at the file instead of at him. That's all I need is for him to read the attraction on my face, and this whole thing will be over before it even begins. "You're right, Bear. We're here for a job. So we need to do it and then get back to Whiskey Run."

I open my file and start reading it and try to memorize everything I'm going to need to know for this mission. As I read through it, I call out some minor details that I'm catching on that maybe both of us need to be aware of. "It says we have two daughters." I pull out the photos and show him. "Chelsea and Caitlin are their names." He looks at the images and then at me. "Thank God they got your good looks," he says, and I don't know which one of us is more surprised by that compliment. It causes a weird flutter in my belly, and I take the photos and put them back in the file.

I clear my throat and keep reading. "It says we've been married for five years and this is our five-year anniversary trip. We're staying at the Playa Del Sol resort." I smirk. "Fancy. And looks like we got invited to a poker game tonight after dinner."

I keep reading and mention to Bear, "It looks like Dylan has planted who we are and that we're looking to get into the business." I look over at Bear. "So I guess that means you are interested in getting into their business." I say the words without actually saying it. I don't want to talk about human trafficking on the plane, but Bear knows exactly what I'm saying.

He gets a disgusted look on his face and shrugs his shoulders. "I know it's not ideal, but if it means that we can save any of these women, then it's worth it."

I nod in agreement with him and then go back to reading. "It says we're just here to learn the process and go home."

Bear grunts, and for the first time, I agree with him. I can't imagine just leaving knowing everything that we're probably going to see tonight. "I know. Me too."

"Huh?" he asks, surprised.

I just smirk at him. "I've learned to read your grunts, Bear. That one you just gave me was, 'Yeah, that's what we're supposed to do—just watch—but I'm not happy about it.'"

He nods his head, and his look softens. I don't think he's used to people speaking Bear. "What else?" he asks.

"Well, there's a list of names and different things like that. People that we'll probably meet or run into, who we should avoid." I point to the names on the paper, not wanting to say them out loud. But when I look at him, he's not looking at the paper. He's staring at me, and his look is guarded again. He's looking at me like it's painful to even be talking with me. I close the file and fold my hands together on top of it. "You do know that you're going to have to act like you like me, right?" I ask him.

His eyes don't shift from where they're trained on my face. His facial features don't change at all; he's just looking at me blankly and shrugs. It doesn't leave me feeling very confident.

"I can do that," he says.

I nod and laugh, even though a part of me wants to cry. "So you're telling me you can act like you love me. That I'm your wife you've loved and been faithful to for five years." I shake my head. "You think you can be convincing? Because I have to be honest with you right now, I don't think you're going to be able to pull it off."

He crosses his big, beefy arms across his big chest. I try to ignore the way the stance makes him look even more dominant. "What about you? Can you pull it off? You think people will believe that someone like you is happy with someone like me?"

I jerk, instantly offended. "What do you mean, someone like me?"

He leans forward and whispers, "I mean someone like you. A hot-ass stubborn woman that could have any man you want. You think people will believe you're happily married to me?" He points at himself with his thumb.

Damn. It takes everything in me not to crawl into his lap right now. Any woman would be blessed to be with Bear. And it won't be hard at all for me to pretend anything with this man. I pull at my shirt around my neck because suddenly the temperature of the plane just got way hotter. "Yeah," I squeak and then clear my voice. "I can."

His eyes never leave mine. "Well, this I can't wait to fuckin' see."

Instead of getting into another argument with him, I just roll my eyes and turn back to the file as if I'm studying it. I want to kick myself. I always go for the emotionally unavailable men, and of course of all the men in Whiskey Run I like the one man that shows zero emotion. He looks as if he's impatient just sitting next to me. How the hell are we going to pull this off? There's no way people are going to believe we're happily married. Not like this.

4

BEAR

How can a two-hour plane ride seem twice as long? She thinks it's going to be hard to act like I like her when I'm doing my best to contain myself sitting next to her this whole damn time.

And the whole entire time, I held myself back, stopping myself from reaching for her hand, her arm, or even her thigh. I want my hands on her. God help me, when she was talking, I could barely pay attention to what she was saying, because the only thing that I was focused on was her lips. Fuck, they're so kissable.

We're walking off the plane, down the hallway, and I'm letting her walk in front of me. She has an independent streak a mile long, and I'm trying not to infringe on that, so I've been walking behind her and just watching her hips sway back and forth.

She stops suddenly and turns, frowning at me. She takes the few steps back to me and grabs my hand, threading our fingers together. I look down at our intertwined hands and have to remind myself to breathe.

She leans in, and her voice is soft as she whispers in my ear, "We're supposed to appear as a happily married couple, Bear. Right now you look as if you're going to kill someone."

I pull back to look at her, and there's a man over her shoulder. He's been beside us since we got off the plane and hasn't been able to keep his eyes off Samantha since. It's driving me crazy, and it doesn't take much, but I'm already to my breaking point. I look at the guy and tell him, "Look, buddy, I suggest you stop staring at my wife and move on."

The man notices me for the first time, which is hard to believe because I'm easily noticeable for how much bigger I am compared to others. His eyes widen, and he takes off in the opposite direction. I feel a little better, but not much. I have a feeling this won't be the first time I have to run someone off on this mission.

Samantha gasps next to me, but I don't care. I'm not going to stand by and let someone stare her like that. I don't want anybody's eyes on her but me. I know that makes me territorial, and she probably doesn't fucking appreciate that, but I just can't do it. I'm seething and about to cause a scene when she pulls me to her. Her tight body is pressed against mine, and I swear I've forgotten my name, not to mention what it is I'm mad about. She pats me on the chest. Her hand is warm right over my heart, and I know that she can feel it thundering underneath her palm.

I'm surprised when I look at her face because she's not mad. If anything, she's smiling from ear to ear. "Better. I mean, you don't have to scare people off, but well played."

She pulls my hand to lead me to the exit of the airport, and I follow behind her like a lovestruck little puppy.

She thought I was joking. She thought that it was all for show, that I ran that guy off to be convincing or whatever. Fuck, that's the furthest thing from the truth. I felt that insane, territorial jealous feeling coursing all the way through my body. I wasn't joking in the least. I won't stand by and let some man look at her the way that asshole was. This is probably going to be one of the hardest missions I've ever been on in my life. I'm going to have to form a whole new level of self-control.

5
SAMANTHA

THREE HOURS LATER, AND I'M STILL FANNING myself. I stare at the king-sized bed in the middle of the room and know that there is no way I'm going to survive this mission. I may have lived through combat. I may have survived being shot at in enemy territory, but I will not survive sleeping in the same bed as Bear. My eyes flick to him sitting on the balcony. As soon as we walked into the room, he took one look at the bed, dropped the bags that he insisted on carrying, and then went straight outside the balcony door.

I expected him to get on his phone or something like that, but he didn't. And I've been watching him. I hate to admit it, but I thought maybe he wanted to check out the women on the beach or by the pool, both which we have a great view of. I've not heard of Bear hooking up with anyone—heck, for all I know he could have a girlfriend or fiancée at home. But I don't think that's the case. He has sat in the same position ever since he got out there, staring at his hands the whole time, playing with the wedding band on his finger.

Instantly I look down at the big rock on my mine. I still can't believe that he went and bought the wedding rings. I have so many questions about it. Like what was he thinking? Who was he thinking about? What does he plan to do with them after this? Surely, he'll just return them, right? I shake my head and sit on the chair in the corner of the room. From here I have a perfect view of the bed and of Bear. Instantly a thousand images start to play in my mind, and it's all sweaty bodies, my legs wrapped around his waist, his big hands holding mine to the bed. I have a full body tremble and shake my head to try to get the images out.

I jump up and decide that I just need to go on about my business. He can sit out there and stew on whatever it is he's thinking about. I'm going to shower and get ready for dinner. I take my time, and at the end of it, I turn the faucet to cold to help calm my nerves. It isn't until I'm done that I realize I have not brought in any clothes.

With a towel wrapped around me, I walk out and head straight for the bags on the bed. It isn't until I'm bent over, digging in the bag that I realize Bear has taken up his position in the chair in the corner of the room. He's leaning forward with his elbows on his knees, openly staring at me.

"I'm sorry, I forgot to take my bag into the bathroom," I tell him.

His gaze goes down my body all the way to my pink toes and then back up again. I wish I could see what he's thinking. His face is completely guarded. He grunts something, but I can't make out what it is. I almost ask him to repeat it, but I can't get past the thickness of my throat. He has me all turned on because he keeps watching me. I don't think it's my imagination or maybe it's just hopeful thinking on my part, but my whole body comes alive underneath his gaze.

I grab a pair of panties and a sundress and hold it up, then drop it quickly, realizing I'm showing him my panties. I barely resist smacking my hand across my forehead. *You are such a fool, Samantha.*

That's it, just show the man your panties. Geez, you'd think I'd never been around a good-looking man before.

I walk quickly away back into the bathroom and shut the door. I dress quickly, take a few breaths, and then walk back out into the room, hoping that we can disregard and forget everything that just happened moments ago. As soon as I'm back into the bedroom, he stands up, and for a second I think he's walking toward me, and I suck in a breath and hold it. But he doesn't come to me. Instead, he goes to the bed and grabs his bag and walks past me, completely ignoring me.

Bear

MY HAND IS on Samantha's back as I guide her to the table for dinner. We are in the restaurant at the resort, and I'm making sure to stick as close as possible to her. Usually I can handle these things in stride and take notice of everything without it being obvious, but not now. Not with Samantha's safety at stake. She leans toward me. "Are you okay?"

I nod and help her to her seat, holding the chair out for her. I release her long enough to go to my seat and sit down next to her. I stretch my legs out until my knee touches her outer thigh.

The server comes to us immediately, and we order our drinks.

"Are you ready to order also or should I come back?"

I don't even think Sam looked at the menu and am about to send the server away when Sam starts to order. "I'll take the salmon and rice. Side salad with honey mustard on the side."

"Very well, and you, sir?" the server asks, turning to me.

"Filet, rare. Baked potato, loaded, and I'll take a salad too. Smother it in ranch."

The server doesn't even flinch, simply nods and takes the menus.

"Smother it in ranch? Really?"

I resist leaning toward her with my elbows on the table. "Yeah. If I'm going to eat healthy, I need to balance it out a little."

She smirks, and her eyes light up. Fuck, I love making her smile. Especially since it seems that most the time, I'm pissing her off.

As if realizing she's let her guard down, the smile falls from her face, and she sits back in the chair, putting distance between us. There's an uncomfortable silence, and I know I can't just sit here and stare at her, so I let my gaze sweep the room. I know that I'm looking at everyone as if they're a threat, quite possibly because they probably are. Sam leans across the table. "I don't know why you insisted on coming. You're going to ruin the whole operation," she hisses under her breath.

I press my lips together. And here I thought it was going so well. "I'm sorry."

She just shakes her head. "I don't know how Nash thought this was a good idea."

I lean up, and we're so close that to others, it probably looks like we're just whispering sweet things to each other, but that couldn't be further from the truth. "Is it so unbelievable that someone like you would be with someone like me? I'm sorry if me being here instead of Logan offends you so much."

She leans back in her chair and looks at me as if she's just seeing me for the very first time. She crosses her arms over her chest, making it obvious how mad she is. And then as if realizing what she's done, she releases her hands, leans across the table, and puts one hand on top of mine. She's gritting her teeth, and I know we may not appear to be the perfect couple, but at least she's trying. I probably need to do the same.

It isn't long before the waiter brings back our salads, and we both start to eat. She finishes her first bite, opens her mouth to say something, and closes it again.

Finally, I can't take it any longer. "Just say it. I know you're dying to."

She smiles sweetly, and I'm expecting something smart-alecky to come out of her pretty mouth. "No, it's not hard to imagine us together. I mean, you have to know you're like every woman's dream, Bear."

I drop my fork, and the loud noise of it hitting my plate has the people at the next table spinning around to look at us. I smile at them while picking the fork back up, and then I look Sam square in the eye. There's no way she's serious. I'm just about to call her out when she leans forward.

"That's right, Bear. I've thought about us— about me and you together. I mean, I know we can never act on it since we work together and all, but yeah, it's not hard to imagine the two of us together."

She pauses, and the words sink in. I swallow as my trousers get tighter. She moves in even farther,

her breasts being pushed up as she leans on the table. "But obviously you can't. You can barely look at me. I talk, and it's like you wish I'd shut up." She lets out a disappointed sigh. "So however you feel about me, that's fine, but I'm here to do a job, and part of that is us being a happily married couple, so that's what I'm going to do."

She forks a piece of her salmon, and I'm waiting for her to put it between her lips, but she surprises me and holds it out to me. "Here, try this."

Now I typically don't like salmon. I eat steak and potatoes, but I'm realizing that Sam could hold out something gross like octopus or squid or something like that, and I'd probably eat it. I lean forward and take a bite. She starts to withdraw her hand, and I grab it. With my other hand, I grab the chair she's sitting in and pull her closer to me. It makes a loud noise, but I don't even care. I need her closer. Her eyes widen and start to sparkle. Sam may say she's independent, but she likes this; she likes me manhandling her like this.

I take the fork from her hand and pierce a piece of steak from my plate and hold it out to her lips. She takes a bite, and right then I swear that's what I want from now on. I want to feed her for the rest of our lives. If it was possible, I would find a way for her to be in my lap when doing so.

There's a calmness that comes over me at her admission. I never dreamt or even let myself hope that she could possibly have feelings for me too, but I know I heard her right. She admitted that she's thought about us, and just knowing that makes it seem as if everything is going to be okay.

We continue to eat our meal, but I hold her hand the rest of the time. When she gets up to go powder her nose, I get up too.

"What are you doing?" she asks.

"I'm going with you."

She shakes her head, laughing that cute way that she does when I'm being overprotective. It's like she doesn't think she should like it, but obviously she does. "I can go on my own."

I hold on to her hand tightly. She doesn't have a clue. But there's no way I'm letting her out of my sight. Knowing that the country's most wanted human traffickers are here on this property, in this resort with their eyes most likely on us—yeah, there's no fucking way I'm letting her go. There's no way I would ever risk anything happening to her.

I lean over and press my lips to her neck. She

arches her chin as she sucks in a breath. I whisper in her ear, "I'm not letting you out of sight."

Thank fuck, she agrees, "Okay." I sign the ticket with our room number and then follow her out of the restaurant. Thank goodness we still have the poker game to go to and a room full of people because I don't trust myself to be alone with her. Not right now. Fuck, probably ever.

6

SAMANTHA

We arrive at the poker tournament, and Bear is completely hovering over me. I can't even complain about it because I've already told him that he needed to show me some affection. So instead of trying to resist or guard my heart like I should be doing, I'm just going to bask in it.

We sit down at a blackjack table, and I win the first hand.

"You're pretty good at this," Bear says.

I just shrug off the compliment. "Yeah, well. I've had a lot of experience. People think they can play me, and I'm just going to lose or fold. I've learned to get better." I shrug my shoulders. "What else do you do when you have a lot of time on your hands?"

He looks at me knowingly. I'm sure when he served in the Army, he and his crew played cards when they had down time.

I try to be humble about it, but after my five-game winning streak, we start to draw attention to ourselves. I can tell by the look on Bear's face that he doesn't know if that's a good or a bad thing.

"Little lady. You are one lucky woman," says the man sitting next to me. I take a drink of Bear's beer as he leans in closer and puts his hand on my thigh. I cover his hand with my own and smile at the other man.

"Well, thank you. I appreciate that. My name is Samantha, and this is my husband Liam." I gesture over my shoulder at Bear, and at this point, I can feel all the body heat from him as Bear has his body pressed to my side.

The guy nods. "They call me Tex. But no introductions are necessary; I know all about the two of you."

I giggle and try not to blanche at the ditzy sound I make. I blink my eyes and look as innocent as I can. "Oh you do, do you?"

The man nods and waves over a waitress. "Get two shots of tequila for my friends."

The waitress nods. "Right away, sir."

"Well, what about you? You're not going to drink with us?" I turn so I'm completely facing the man next to us. I figure if he knows who we are already then he's someone that I want to keep an eye on; however, I don't recognize him from the dossier Dylan had prepared for us.

"Nope, not me. I can't drink the stuff. I stick to whatever's on draft," he says, holding up an iced mug.

The server comes and sets the drinks in front of Bear and me. I throw it back and then chase it with the Coke that I have sitting in front of me. The man next to me looks impressed and orders another.

Bear starts to hold his hand up, and I grab it and kiss his palm. Looking into his eyes, I know he's trying to tell me to chill out, but I try to reassure him by pulling his arm around my shoulder. "It's okay, sweetie. I haven't been able to let loose in a while. Let me have some fun." I say it in the most fun-loving voice I can muster. I'm sure the man sitting next to me thinks I'm some kind of dingbat, but all I'm going to do is play the part.

When the next shots come, I drink it, chasing it with the Coke. The man is still smiling at me, and I start to lay it on thick and really flirt with him. He's eating it up and laughing and having a good time, which is exactly what I'm shooting for.

"So what are your plans while you're in town?" he asks.

Bear puts his hands on my shoulders. "Just spending time with my wife." He says it simply, but he stresses the words *my wife*.

I lean into his touch. The possessive way that he says *wife* sends a thrill down my spine.

Bear stands up, and I topple on my heels when I stand up too. I'm playing the part of the inebriated wife that's just looking for a good time. Bear's jaw clenches. "I think it's time that we go back to our room." He nuzzles my neck, and I turn to face him.

"I like how you're thinking, hubby." I take a step and pretend to sway on my feet. The man reaches out to steady me at the same time Bear does. Bear tucks me under his arm, and when we're about to walk away, the man stops us.

"There's a party tomorrow night. I'm thinking it's one you would like to attend." He wiggles his eyebrows, and I swear if it's the kind of party I think it is, I'll throw up in my mouth a little bit.

I keep the smile on my face, though. It's too important, and I know I can't lose character now. I'm surprised that it was that easy. "We would love to," I answer him without even looking at Bear for confirmation.

We walk out, and I stay tucked under Bear's arm until we get off the elevator and are walking to our room. It's then that I start walking normally. Bear gets a surprised look on his face. He looks at my legs and then back up at me. "Wait... what?"

I pat him on the stomach. "It's an old party trick. I didn't drink any of that. I pretended to chase it with my Coke, but I was actually spitting it in the cup."

Bear laughs as he unlocks the hotel room. "Remind me never to challenge you at a drinking game."

I walk past him into the room. "Yeah, because you'd lose all your money."

He shakes his head and grips the back of his neck. "Yeah, I have a feeling I'd lose more than just money."

The door shuts behind us, and before I can ask him what that means, he's already dialing his phone. "I'm going to call this in. Nash will want to know."

I grab pajamas from the bag and go into the bathroom to change. I take out a makeup remover pad and wipe my face quickly, anxious to get back out there and hear the conversation.

"Yeah, I can't believe it either," I hear Bear say, "but Sam did an awesome job, and she's the reason we got in the door."

I try not to let the shock show on my face. He's giving me all the credit.

Nash says something else, and then I hear Bear say, "I know we were only here for intel, but we can't pass up this opportunity."

Damn straight we can't. I lean against the wall outside of the bathroom and brush my teeth and watch Bear pace back and forth. A part of me wants to take the phone from him and demand Nash listen to reason, but I know I can't do that. Bear has worked with Nash for a long time. I'm sure he knows what he's doing.

They seem to go back and forth forever, and I go and rinse my mouth out, and when I come out, Bear is off the phone. He looks at me and notices the question on my face. "Yeah, they're going to send backup."

"Good job," I tell him, thankful that he was able to talk them into pursuing this.

I sit on the edge of the bed. Bear is standing there in his dress pants and buttoned-up shirt that's tight across the arms and chest. I hadn't thought of it, but I'd say it's hard to find shirts that fit him. "You're the one that did a good job. I don't think we would've got that invite if it wasn't for you." I shrug off his compliment. "You done in there?" he asks, pointing at the bathroom.

I nod, and he walks that way. When he comes back out, he's in shorts and a T-shirt. I'd be willing to bet the man is used to sleeping naked, and the clothes are for my benefit. I've moved to under the covers, and he goes straight for the couch. "What are you doing?"

"I'm going to sleep on the couch." He points at the little two-seater couch, and I know there's no way he's going to fit.

I throw back the covers. "I wasn't even thinking. I'll sleep on the couch. I'm smaller than you are."

He shakes his head. "I'm not going to have you sleep on the couch."

I stand up and start to move that way. "I can sleep on the couch."

He grits his teeth. "There's no way I'm going to sleep in that bed and have you sleep on the couch."

I shake my head in frustration. "That's ridiculous. I've slept out on the ground before. I can sleep on a small couch."

He's all stubborn and crosses his arms over his chest. "I'm not going to let you sleep on the couch."

I throw my hands up in the air. "We're grown adults. This bed is huge." I point at the massive bed.

"I'm huge," he says, unfurling his arms.

My thoughts go dirty in an instant. I've already pictured it in my mind a thousand times wondering exactly how big he is. *Geez, don't go there, Sam. Get your mind out of the gutter*.

"Well, I'm not lying down until you get into that bed." I wait for him to refuse, but he surprises me when he goes to the opposite side and lies down.

I then crawl back into my side and lie down. Even though the bed really is big, it seems so much smaller with him in it next to me. It's obvious he's trying to keep his distance, but I swear I can feel his body heat.

I toss and turn, trying to get comfortable, finally coming to a rest. I have my body turned toward him and my head on the pillow looking at him. "Tell me about yourself."

He grunts, and instantly I know he's not going to answer. I try not to voice my disappointment as I turn away from him. "I'm sorry. Obviously, you're a private person."

I hear him take a deep breath in the dark room, and then he starts to talk. "I was in the Army for a long time, since I was eighteen. I was on my second tour and was in Iraq when I became a prisoner of war. Nash and Walker are the ones that saved me. And it was shortly after that that I started working for them."

I roll back over toward him. "You were a prisoner of war?" How could I have not known that? Nobody has ever said a thing to me about him.

"Yeah. It was years ago, but I still have nightmares about it sometimes."

I reach for him in the darkness as he continues talking. "My ex-wife cheated on me while I was a POW. Needless to say, that's why she's my ex. I haven't trusted or dated anyone since."

"What a bitch," I say. I mean what kind of woman could do that? It's horrible. I feel physically ill just imagining what all Bear has gone through.

He laughs, and the sound surprises me. "Tell me about you." Obviously he's done talking about himself, and even though I have a thousand questions I want to ask, I don't. I tell him about serving with Walker on a mission in Belize. I talk to him about how I've always had to fight for my position, which is why I'm always trying to prove myself.

His voice is normally deep and thick, but it seems even more so in the dark room. "I think you've already proven yourself to all of us. There's no doubt that you can do your job and do it well. I think all the guys have learned to trust and have faith in you."

His words send a thrill through my body, not only because he's telling me exactly what I'm striving for, but also just the fact that he feels that way too.

It isn't long before I'm yawning in the bed next to him, and he turns away, rolling toward the opposite direction. "Get some sleep. I have a feeling that tomorrow is going to be a big day."

For once, I do as he asks without arguing with him. But I have no doubt that I'm going to be dreaming of a certain husky man that has somehow come to take over every thought I have.

7
BEAR

I'M DRINKING COFFEE ON THE BALCONY WHEN SAM comes to stand at the door. She looks beautiful, all soft and rumpled. I have an internal fight with myself not to get up, throw her over my shoulder, and take her back to bed. When I woke up this morning, she was on top of me, her hips pushing against my hard cock. Getting out of that bed was the hardest thing that I've ever had to do. There's a part of me that wishes I was the type of man that could have just pushed her to her back, woken her up with a fiery kiss, and seen where it would lead.

But there's no part of me that wants to take advantage of her. When and if she ever comes to me, I want her to do it of her own volition.

She stretches, and her hard nipples press against

the T-shirt she has on. "What do you want to do today?"

"Whatever you want," I tell her. Heck, she could say she wants to go swim with sharks right now, and I'd follow her into the water.

She leans against the door frame. "How about swimming and lounging around the pool? It would be good to be seen around the resort... out and about."

I have to agree with her on that. We can't stay holed up in this room. Not with that big bed and all the dirty thoughts stirring in my head. "Sounds good. Let's do that."

She smiles widely, and it's nice that something as easy as that makes her happy. She gets ready, and then so do I. We stop at the coffee shop in the lobby for her to get a latte and a pastry, then head out to the pool. It's already starting to fill up even this early in the day. There's a swim-up bar, and I see people that were at the poker tournament last night already sitting at the bar drinking.

The resort is beautiful, making me wish we were here for different reasons than the one we have. It's hard to be happy knowing what's happening in this very hotel.

I take my shirt off and toss it onto one of the

chairs. Samantha gasps behind me. "Bear," she says.

I turn, quickly ready to fight off anything but then realize that she was surprised by the scars that she saw on my back. I'd completely forgotten all about them. She walks up to me and puts her hand on my chest. She's real quiet. "Is that from...?"

She doesn't have to continue. I know what she's asking and that she's referring to my time as a POW. I nod, and her hand slides from my chest to my back, and she rests her head on my chest. She kisses me there on my bare skin because that's all she can reach. "I'm so sorry. Bear, I'm so sorry." She says it over and over, and I know that she is sincere.

I reach down and cup her chin, lifting her face to look at me. "It's not your fault." She lifts her shoulders. "I know it's not, but I can't imagine what you went through then and what you came home to."

There are tears in her eyes, and I'm touched by the emotion on her face. I had worried that I'd regret telling her, and that maybe she would think I'm weak. But obviously she doesn't.

I lean down. "Can I kiss you, Sam?" I say it almost breathlessly.

She nods and smiles. "I mean, we are supposed to be playing like we're married."

I stop then, realizing what we're doing and where we're at. For just a second, I had forgotten that this is all fake. That here we are Samantha and Liam, not Sam and Bear. Instead of kissing her lips like I want to so badly, I kiss her on the forehead and release the hold I have on her.

She's surprised; I can see it in her eyes. I wanted more than just a forehead kiss, but how can I do more, if she thinks it's all fake and everything I'm feeling is real?

She gets herself together and walks over to her chair, the one next to mine, and takes off her wrap. She's standing in a white bikini that leaves very little to the imagination. Her breasts are round and full, and her waist and ass have the perfect amount of curviness. My mouth starts to water, and I can't take my eyes off her. I sit down before I fall down. "Is that the only bathing suit you have?" I ask her through gritted teeth.

She nods, looking down at herself. "Yeah, what's wrong with it?"

I shake my head. "Nothing, if you want every man looking at you. I won't be able to do my job for fending off crazed men."

She laughs as if I'm joking, and I'm not. One look at her would cause even the saintliest of men to turn bad.

She sits down on the chair and pulls out lotion to start wiping along her legs. "You can actually be sweet sometimes, Bear."

I growl at her, and she laughs again. She has no idea what she's playing with. My eyes are glued to her body. She doesn't realize that if some guy gets in his head that he can touch her that I will straight-up kill him. I will end his life and not even think about it.

She leans back and pulls her glasses down over her eyes. I need to get into the pool and cool off, but there's no way I'm going to leave her here alone. So instead, I sit down in the chair next to her, put my glasses down over my eyes, and turn my head toward her. She can say what she wants—hell, I don't even care if she sees me staring at her because there's nothing else I'd rather be looking at than her.

Sam

HE'S WATCHED me for the last hour, and my whole body feels as if it's on fire. There's no doubt that there's a wet spot in the panties of my bathing suit. I slide my legs together on the chair, feeling the friction between my thighs. This feeling that Bear ignites inside of me is crazy and confusing. I know it's a bad idea, but I also know that no man has ever made me senseless like this just from a look. It leaves me with an uncontrollable urge of wanting something and not knowing if I can ever have it.

I sit up in my chair, toss my glasses down, and unsteadily stand on my feet. He jumps up quickly beside me. "Where are you going?"

I laugh. "Relax. I'm getting in to cool off a little." I have a feeling that's the only option I have. I need to cool down, and sitting next to him while his eyes roam my body, always looking and never touching, is not helping.

He follows behind me and stands waist deep in the pool. Every woman around is looking at him, but I can't be mad about it. I mean, how can you not look at him? I could spend hours just looking at him, and with his arms crossed over his chest and that look on his face, his eyes hidden behind his sunglasses, he looks even more sexy.

As he stands watching me, I dive into the water

and swim a few laps. I try to think of anything but him. Him in those black swim shorts that show off his muscular hairy legs. Him with his big, bulgy muscles. Damn, him with his overprotective attitude. After a few laps, I swim up to him, breathless. I can easily blame my panting on the workout, but in part it's him also. I stand up out of the water, and his jaw tightens. The possessive look he gives me is like a jolt to my system. "Well, you have the possessive husband look down. There's no way a man is going to come talk to me like this," I tell him, waving my hand up and down in front of him.

He tilts his head, pushes his glasses up, and rests them on top of his head. He stares at me without even blinking. "Does that bother you that I'm not going to let some man come up and talk to you?"

I shrug, not wanting him to know exactly what that possessive glint in his eye does to me. I swear he's claimed me with that look and doesn't even realize it. "No, but I'm not going to get any closer or get intel if you're hovering over me."

He reaches out like he's going to grab me but then stops suddenly and drops his hands at his sides. "That's not the mission. You are not the target. You will not be the target." He's staring at me fiercely, and I know I've hit a button. This isn't the reaction from just some man I work with. Bear may not want to admit it, but there's more to this relationship between us.

I tilt my head back to look up at him, and for the first time, I wish I had my sunglasses still on. I'm almost embarrassed to ask, but I'm going to do it anyway. I probably shouldn't, but I can't stop myself. "Can I ask you something?"

He looks at me skeptically. "Yes."

Before I can talk myself out of it, I blurt out, "This morning when I woke up—" and then I stop, suddenly not able to put the words out there.

He stiffens, and then I realize that maybe it wasn't my imagination. He's obviously not going to make a move, and I want to know something. I lean toward him, and my nipples pebble just from being this close to him. I'm so close. I take a deep breath, and I can feel them pucker against his chest. "I had a dream that something happened with us."

He puts his hands on my shoulders. I don't know if he's trying to pull me toward him or push me away. I don't think he does, either. He holds on to me firmly, though. "I didn't take advantage of you. I wouldn't do that."

I almost laugh. I already know that without him

having to tell me, but I don't think he understands what I'm trying to say. "I know you wouldn't, but would it be taking advantage if I wanted it?" As soon as the words are out, I hold my breath, waiting for his reaction.

He grits his teeth, and I lose my bravery and start to walk away. When I get to the edge of the pool, he grabs on to my waist to hold me. He pulls me back into the water, and my back is fitted against his chest. "Fuck, Sam. You might as well not have anything on." I look down at my hard nipples and gasp before covering my chest. The bathing suit does nothing to hide my attraction to Bear, and obviously a white bathing suit wasn't the right choice. I put my head in my hand, just thinking about him looking at me from behind. I can just imagine what he saw.

"Stay here," he demands. He gets out of the pool, and my gaze follows him all the way over to our seats. He grabs a towel, and when he comes back to me, I notice the huge bulge in his shorts. I swallow thickly, my mouth watering. Damn, is that because of me? I get to the water's edge and barely get out of the pool before he's wrapping the towel around me. I mutter "thanks" to him and start to walk away, hoping I can get away and deal with my embarrassment. I've pretty much just thrown myself at him, and even though he's interested, he's not going to act on it.

I'm grabbing my things from the chair and about to walk back to the room when he stops me. "Where are you going?"

I try to hide my emotions and turn to him. "Well, I was trying to cool off, but I don't think it's going to happen." He doesn't say anything, and I throw my hands up in frustration. "I mean, is it just me? Is it one-sided or what? Because damn, Bear, I want you."

His nostrils flare, and he takes a deep breath. He looks almost lethal staring back at me, eating me up with his eyes. I can see the conflict on his face, and then suddenly, he holds his hand out to me. "Come with me."

I know that this is a big decision right now. I can either take his hand and see where he leads me and what could happen between the two of us, or I could live in my safe little bubble and wonder what could have been. It's not even a hard decision to make. I put my hand in his, and he pulls me against him. We walk toward the hotel, through the lobby and to the elevators. I can feel people watching us, but my eyes are on Bear. To anyone else, he looks mad. To me, he looks like a man that is about to lose control.

We're waiting on the elevator, and I'm starting to worry that he hasn't said anything. "Bear...." I start, and he pulls me tighter against him. He positions me in front of him, his hands on my waist, and pulls me back to him. His hard manhood is pressing into my back.

The elevator dings, and when the doors open, we wait for people to get off, and then we walk in. When we're alone inside, I turn in his arms. "Bear..."

He shakes his head. "Sam, I'm barely hanging on here. It wouldn't take much for me to have you stripped and bent over with your ass in the air. Don't tempt me. Wait until we're in our room." He finishes by giving me a smack on my ass, and I huff and turn away from him. So many things are going through my mind. I shouldn't like it, but dang, I like this alpha, take-control side of Bear.

He pulls me back against him, and I can feel his hard length pulsating against me. My whole body trembles at what is going to come when we get to the room.

8

BEAR

FROM THE MINUTE SHE SAID SHE WANTED ME, AN uncontrollable urge has taken over me. I wasn't lying to her. I'm barely hanging on here, and I know that nothing is going to satisfy me until I'm balls deep inside her.

With my hand on her lower back, I guide her down the hall. "Are you on the pill?"

She stumbles on her feet, and I hold her up with one arm around her waist. She's staring up at me. "Uh, yeah."

"I'm clean."

She nods. "Me too."

"Good," I grunt. "I want you bare with nothing between us."

"Bear?" She looks at me questioningly. I let her

go to dig the card out of my pocket and unlock the room.

I hold the door open with one hand and guide her in with the other, but I don't let her go far. I grab her, turn her, and lean her against the wall. I pull the towel from her body and let it fall to the floor. She's breathing heavily, her breasts rising and falling, causing her puckered nipples to graze my chest.

"I need you," I grunt, pushing my lower body against her, letting her feel how much I want her.

She whimpers and grinds her hips against me. I know the feeling exactly. She wants to get closer, and so do I.

I kiss her lips, and my hand trails down her neck, across her shoulder, and down the outside of her breast. She arches her back, and I cup her full breast, pushing the thin white material away until I feel her bare in my palm. I trail kisses down her neck to her breasts and suckle her. The need to touch her everywhere takes over, and while my lips move to her other breast, my hand slides under the panties of her bathing suit, through the soft curls at her apex and through her wet, swollen lips. She lifts up on her tiptoes and whimpers.

"Fuck, you're wet." I groan as I about fall to my knees to taste her.

She grips on to my shoulders. "No, Bear. I need you inside me. Please?"

I rise up and pull my swim shorts to my knees. My cock is hard between us, and I lift her up in my arms, leaning her back against the wall. With one hand on her back and the other around my girth, I guide myself into her.

She's so fucking tight, but I push into her until she's completely seated on my thick, rigid pole.

Her fingers splay across my chest, and she grips me there. "Please, don't stop."

I grunt and start to move. In and out of her, my hands on her hips, I move her up and down. Her head falls back and bangs on the wall, but she doesn't even wince.

"Look at me," I tell her.

She lifts her head and stares at me with hooded blue eyes.

"Can you come like this? I need you to come."

She huffs. "I've never... with someone else. It's okay," she says.

I stop and gape at her. What kind of selfish bastards...

Fuck it, there's no way I won't make her come.

I lift her off the wall and move her to the bed, laying her back as gently as possible. Still connected, I move in and out of her, using one hand to hold her open and the other to stroke her clit.

She moans and grips on to my forearm. She's shaking her head, but I'm not stopping. In and out, my hips gyrate against hers. I increase the pressure on her clit until she's clawing at me. She's so damn close. "Don't stop," she begs.

"I'm not stopping, honey. Not until you come for me."

"Oh...oh..." I know I'm hitting the right spot. I increase the pressure on her clit and reach for her waist to hold her in place.

"Come for me, baby. I need to feel you explode around me. Milk me, Sam. I need to fill you up."

"Arrrrgh!" she yells as her body starts to writhe uncontrollably underneath me. Every muscle is pulled taut, and her eyes are wide open in astonishment. She's too tight. Too hot and too wet. I bellow, way louder than I probably should, but I can't hold back. I've never felt anything so perfect before in my life.

I come then, until I've completely filled her up.

We're both panting and trying to catch our

breath. I pull away and grab the towel I took off her earlier and clean myself off before going to the bathroom to grab one for her. When I come out of the bathroom, she's already standing up with my T-shirt over her head.

I stop in front of her. "As much as I like seeing you in my shirt, I like you better with nothing."

She won't look at me. As a matter of fact, she's looking everywhere but at me. "Look at me, Sam."

She blushes, obviously remembering just seconds ago when I said those exact words to her, but I was buried deep in her pussy at the time.

She looks at me with bright red cheeks. "What?"

"You're wasting your time covering yourself up. I'm going to have you again."

Her hand goes to my chest like that's going to stop me. "Bear."

I shrug. "What? It's the truth. That pussy is golden. I'm going to need more."

She laughs as if I'm joking. "I see, so basically what you're saying is you're just after my body."

Without even thinking about it, I tug the shirt off her, pick her up, and lay her back down on the bed and follow after her. "I want it all."

"Bear..." she says, searching my eyes.

I cup her face in my hand and hold her gaze with my own. "I want it all, Sam. This is nice. Fuck, this was better than I dreamed about. But it's not all I want. I want all of you."

I can tell she's trying to figure out if I'm serious, so I don't even blink. If she looks in my eyes, she'll see exactly what I'm telling her. There's no way she can't see how I feel about her.

She pushes me backwards, and for just a minute, I worry that she's pushing me off her. At least until she swings her leg over and straddles my waist. I grab on to her hips, and my cock is already lengthening, ready for round two. She must feel it against her ass because she rocks backwards and nudges me. "You have to be kidding me."

I shrug. "You're going to find out sooner or later. I can just hear your name and I'm hard. So you, naked on top of me, it's definitely going to happen."

She reaches behind herself and wraps her hand around my girth. I groan as she tightens her hold on me. "Hmmm, I might like this side of you, Bear."

She leans down and kisses me, which is a good thing. It wouldn't take much for me to tell her that I love her and want her to have my babies... and I don't think she's ready for that.

9
SAM

"You're staying here."

I turn and look at him, knowing I didn't hear what I thought I heard. My body is still vibrating from earlier, and obviously it's messed with my hearing. "What did you just say?"

He walks toward me, and I know that look on his face. The bad thing about it is that I know it's going to be hard to say no to Bear. Already, I can feel myself wanting to give him everything he wants. But I've worked too hard for where I am in life; I can't just give up my job and my dreams because he thinks he needs to protect me. And then it hits me. I put my hand on his chest to stop him from coming any closer. "You don't think I can take care of myself?"

He puts his hand over mine as if he's holding it over his heart. "Yes, I do. That's not even a question. I told you that you've proven yourself to me and everyone else. You're a badass, Sam. There's no doubt about it. But what I'm saying is —" He stops and shakes his head. "Fuck, I don't even know what I'm saying. I know I can't keep you here or in a bubble. I..." He exhales deeply and searches my face. "I just can't lose you, that's all."

And just like that, I go from being pissed off and ready to tell him what he can do with that bossy attitude to now I want to just stay in this room and kiss him and let him hold me. "This is my job, Bear. I have to do it."

He's nodding before I even get it all out. "I know that. But I need you to stay by my side. No leaving it for any reason, not even to go to the ladies' room."

I smirk, like he's joking, and he just shrugs. "You think I'm joking? Try it and I'll just follow you in there."

I pat his chest and lean up to kiss him. "Got it. Pee before I get there."

I start to pull away, and he stops me, gathering me in his arms. "We going to talk about what happened?"

I look over at the bed with the tousled sheets, and my body starts to heat all over. "What's there to talk about?"

He's searching my face as if trying to figure out what I'm thinking. I shrug my shoulders as if the last few hours, he hadn't completely and unequivocally made me a lust-filled woman that just wants more. More kisses, more love, more touches. Heck, I want more of anything that includes Bear. But I also know I don't want to scare him off. "I'm a big girl, Bear. You don't have to worry that I'm going to try and tie you down or anything..."

I try to say it lightly, and I'm looking everywhere but at him. His silence has me pulling away from him and walking over to my high-heeled shoes by the chair. I sit down and start to pull them on. When I finally get them on, I try to keep myself guarded and look up at him. "You ready?"

"Yeah, I'm ready," he says, hands in his front pockets.

I try not to let on that I'm disappointed. It's not like I expected him to confess his undying love to me, but I guess I expected something because the discontent settles in my belly.

I nod and am about to walk past him when he

stops me. "So we're going to talk about this after, but there's something you need to know..."

I shake my head, really not wanting to get into it now. I can already feel tears threatening to break free. He moves and blocks my path, gripping my chin to look up at him. "Honey, you may not want to tie me down, but you've already got me tied in knots. I'm claiming you, Sam. You're mine now."

My eyes flick up to his. "But..." There's so many things I could say—*We work together, We haven't known each other that long*—but I don't get any of it out.

He leans down and kisses me until my toes start to curl. Only then does he pull back, and I look up at him, no longer trying to hide my feelings. He tucks a piece of hair behind my ear. "There's no buts. You're mine, Sam. The quicker you figure that out, the easier this is going to be."

He lets me go then and walks over to the dresser, opening up a drawer. He turns to me with a small little box in his hand, and I start to freak out. Surely not... He's not going to... But before I start to hyperventilate, he pulls an earpiece out. "Nash and the guys dropped these off while you were in the shower."

I take it from him and tuck it in my ear as he

holds a necklace up in front of me. "Necklace?" I ask.

"Microphone and video," he answers.

I nod as he puts it around my neck and clasps it. I turn when he's done, and he's putting a pin on his shirt that must be his camera and mic.

He pushes a button. "Test. Can you hear me?"

Dylan comes over the line. "Yes. Test 2?"

I nod. "Test 2, can you hear me?" I say.

Dylan comes over the earpiece again. "I can hear you. Now let's go get the bad guy. I have a wife and a new daughter I need to get home to."

I grab my purse, and Bear ushers me out the door. I walk in front of him down the hall, and Logan's voice is loud in my ear. "Damn, Samantha, you are smokin' hot."

I start to stumble on my high heels, and Bear catches me. It's then I realize Logan was able to see me through Bear's camera.

Bear growls and punches the button for the elevator. "Cut that shit out, Logan, or you'll be going home in a body bag."

There's nothing, not a sound, and I turn to look at Bear. I know the guys can see him too, and I'm sure they see the smoldering look he's giving me. I know what's coming next before it even happens.

I hear Logan, Knox, Dylan all on the line, and they start busting Bear's balls. I guess they figure they're safe since it's all over microphone. It's not until Logan starts chanting about Bear and me sitting in a tree and kissing that I start to laugh.

Bear is holding his hand over his camera. "What's that for?"

He grunts. "I don't want them looking at you. Fuck, I don't want anyone looking at you."

I start to laugh. "I like this whole alpha caveman *she's mine* attitude, but if you try peeing on me..."

He laughs then and pulls me against him. "I wouldn't."

I smile up at him. "Are you sure?"

He shakes his head. "I promise, I won't."

"Wait, did Bear just laugh? Was that Liam James I heard laughing?"

We're approaching the first floor now, and I know Bear is over it. "All right, guys, that's enough. Let's get to work so Dylan can get home to Jenna and Jamie."

Everyone quiets just as Bear and I step out of the elevator. We walk through the lobby and are stopped by the man we saw last night. He looks at us. "Follow me."

He leads us through a big open ballroom and then out the back door. Bear's hand tightens on mine, and I smile up at him. I know he's worried, and probably the two of us working this case together causes a little problem, but I refuse to let it hold either of us back. We're going to take care of this, and we'll work the rest out.

The man opens the door of what looks like another big building. It's a nice building, albeit nondescript. He lets us walk in and closes the door behind us. There are people everywhere; if I were guessing, I'd say there's around thirty to forty people easy.

A waitress comes up to Bear and puts a hand on his shoulder. She's young, way too young to probably even be drinking the alcohol she's holding on the tray. "What can I get you?"

Bear is about to pull away from the woman when I reach for a drink. "Thanks. We'll just take these off your hands." I shove a drink in Bear's hand. "Here you go, honey."

With my eyes, I tell him to relax, and he obviously gets the drift because he smiles at the woman. "Thanks, honey. That will be it.... for now."

I can see him cringe as he says it.

"Fuck, she had to be what, fifteen, sixteen?" Logan says.

"Yep," I answer him as I act like I'm talking to Bear. "If that."

"You made it." I recognize the man's voice from last night, and I turn to face him.

I just smile like the ditz he thinks I am, and Bear answers him. "We wouldn't have missed it."

"So the first hour is just mingling. You'll see girls come and go. They all have numbers on their pockets. Just keep in mind what you're wanting. They go fast, and it's highest bidder."

Bear tenses beside me, and I rub my hand up and down his chest. Bear grunts. "Got it."

The man looks at me. "So you're okay with this, honey? You don't mind sharing?"

I do my very best to keep my face relaxed, and without missing a beat, I nod. "Of course not. He's way more man than I can handle. He'll keep us all happy, won't you, sugar?" I ask, looking up at Bear with my eyes wide.

The guy leans toward me, and Bear doesn't even hesitate. He has me pulled into him so quickly I gasp.

The guy looks at Bear before he starts to laugh.

"Well, I guess that answers my question. You don't share her?"

Bear shakes his head. "Never. And I'll kill any man that tries."

I laugh as if Bear's joking, but there's no way the other man doesn't see the tick in his jaw. I wave at the man. "We'll see you later."

When we get far enough away, I hiss up at Bear, "Are you kidding? You're going to blow this."

He's pulling me now. We're walking out of the room and down a hallway. "I don't care, no one is going to—" We get around a corner, and he pushes me against a wall, flattening his body to mine. "No one is going to touch you, Sam. I wasn't lying. I'll kill them. I don't care who they are."

I shake my head. How is this going to work, us working together? "Oh, Bear."

As if he can't control himself, he lifts me up and kisses me deep and thoroughly. I let him, too; there's no way I can turn him away. My body comes alive as my nipples slide across his chest. I moan loudly, and then there's Logan. "Uh, guys, we can hear you."

I try to pull away, but Bear holds me to him. "Fuck off, Logan."

He turns the mic off, and I do the same.

"You're done, Sam. I need you to go to the room. Let me handle this."

My whole body deflates. This is never going to work between us if we can't even handle this case together. "No."

"Sam, listen, I can't put you in this situation, knowing what we know."

I try to shove him away, but he doesn't even budge. "You mean that there's a roomful of sex traffickers in there."

He nods, but I continue. "And a room full of girls that need our help. This is what we're trained to do, Bear. I can do this."

He shakes his head. "I'm not doubting you. I know you can do it. It's not that... Fuck, I'll go to the room too, and we'll let Logan and the guys come in."

I grab on to the front of his shirt and pull him down until we're eye level. "If you were here with Logan or Knox or Aiden, would you go up to your room and hide?"

"I'm not hiding."

I pull him in close enough until I can feel his breath on my cheek. "No. You're not. You're trying to protect me. I can protect myself. If you want there to be a possibility with us when we get home, you have to trust me, you have to believe in me."

"I do, but I can't lose you. I won't lose you."

My heart does a funny pitter-patter, but I can't even think about it now. I nod and cock my head. "Fine, then let's go kick some ass and save some women. Then afterwards we can finish this conversation."

10

BEAR

I WANT TO TAKE HER BACK UP TO THE ROOM SO badly. Even if I only get to hold her, that would be okay because I'd know she's safe. But I know she's right. I'm not the kind of man that can walk away from a woman in need, and from the looks of it, there's quite a few that are in need tonight.

"Fine. We do this. Do you have your piece on you?"

She rolls her eyes, grabs my hand, and brings it down between her legs. I can feel her thigh holster, and fuck if my dick doesn't get hard. She's definitely my kind of woman.

"All right, you ready?"

She nods. "Yeah, but we should probably turn

the mics back on because the guys are probably about to charge in here."

I flip mine on, and so does she. She was right, too, because the guys are on the line arguing and stop suddenly when they hear us. "Fuck, Bear. You can't do that shit," Logan says.

"I know. Sorry, guys, let's do this."

We're walking back into the room, and we listen to Knox go over the plan. "All we need is some surveillance. Get it on film with the women being purchased. FBI is enroute."

"Got it."

I grab on to Sam's waist and do my best to relax as we weave in and out of the crowd of people. We find our way to the front and watch as men find their way to the front to make their bids.

I'm facing one way and Sam the other, doing our best to get it all on film.

An elderly woman makes an announcement that the bidding is starting, and everyone takes their seats. The first woman comes onto the stage, and it's obvious she's young and frightened. "Bidding starts at twenty thousand. She has all her papers. She's fifteen and has been checked by the inhouse doctor. Her hymen is intact."

The bidding starts, and bile rises in my throat.

"Let's end this, guys," I say into the microphone, and as soon as I get the words out, the doors bust open and the room is flooded with FBI and all the members of the ghost team. I'm surprised when I see Nash; he doesn't normally come on missions anymore, but I'm not going to question it. He is the boss.

Sam already has her gun drawn, and I do the same. People are trying to flee and there are people that are fighting back, but they are outnumbered as the local swat team follows in behind the FBI. There's chaos all around us, but it's not long before the people realize they're had and lie down on the ground, waiting to be handcuffed.

The room is on lockdown, and Sam and I move to the back room to help with the women.

We work endlessly through the night, helping the woman get to shelters and working with transport to the local jail facilities until they are all contained.

The FBI captain walks up to us. "The largest number of arrests in one night in Miami history. Good job, men." And then as if he's just noticing Sam, "And lady."

Nash talks to him while the rest of us continue packing up our gear. Someone already packed up

Sam and my stuff from the room, so we're getting on the plane tonight to head home.

"Well, we thank you. The people of Miami thank you." The captain addresses us all again.

We all nod, and Knox, who's closest to him, shakes his hand. "We're just doing our job, sir."

The press is starting to arrive, and that's our cue to get out of here. We load into two vans and go to the airport. We bypass all security and are loaded onto the plane in a whirlwind. As soon as everyone's on board, Aiden has the plane in the air.

Sam is sitting a few seats up from me, and I can't take my eyes off her. At least not until Nash gets up and stands beside me. "Want to debrief me on what happened out there, Bear?"

I nod. "Sure thing, sir."

I stand up, and Sam turns wide eyes to me. I can see the question in her eyes, and I try to smile, even though I'm sure it looks more like a scowl than anything. I hate to explain myself to anyone, and I have a feeling I may not like what Nash is going to say.

Nash takes an aisle seat in the very back of the plane, and I sit in the seat across the aisle from him.

"So..." he starts, and I hold my hand up. I may be a man of few words, but these are important.

"I'm not going to stop seeing her, Nash. If you've got a problem with us dating, tell me now. I'll find another job."

Nash stares at me, and I'm waiting on him to rip my ass or ask me what the hell I'm thinking. But he surprises me. He lets out a breath. "I'm not going to tell you that you can't see her. Fuck, Bear. You find someone you care about, you don't give her up. Trust me, I've made that mistake before, and I wouldn't wish that kind of doom on anyone."

For just a second, Nash looks lost in thought with pain etched on his face. I've never talked to Nash about his personal life, but as long as I've known him, there's never been a woman in the picture. Obviously, there's one I don't know about.

Nash shakes his head. "So, anyway, I get it. But you tell me. I can't lose you or Sam. Are you going to be able to work together and get the job done?"

I grit my teeth. "We'll make it work. There's no other option, Nash."

He seems to weigh my words and finally nods. "Fine, but for a while, you'll be going on separate missions."

"Nash, I don't think..."

Nash holds his hand up. "You trust her?"

I nod.

"You trust the guys?"

Fuck. "Yeah, I do."

"Okay, well, until we smooth out the kinks, that's the way it's going to have to be. Separate missions until we get rules laid out."

"I hate rules," I tell him.

He laughs, and the crew in the front of the plane all turn around to see. "I know you do, but they're needed. You know I'm right, Bear."

"Yes, sir."

***

Sam

"HE'S ALWAYS LIKE THIS. He has to decompress and sort things out in his head after a mission. Usually doesn't say two words to anyone," Knox says while giving me a sympathetic look.

I guess I'm making it obvious the way I'm staring after Bear. He went to the back of the plane and talked to Nash for a while, and when he was done, he walked right past me and sat in the very front seat of the plane.

I know this was a hard mission. No one wants to believe that there are people in this world that would do these kind of things, but I know that since Bear was a POW, he's seen worse. Maybe he's having flashbacks to that. I'm just going to have to be patient.

The flight is quick, and when we land at the base, we all get out. Nash calls a meeting for the next day, and I don't even go inside; I head straight for my car.

I'm embarrassingly slow, carting my luggage behind me, hoping that Bear is going to stop me, but he doesn't.

He's talking to Logan and Knox, and I hear Knox asking if they want to go grab a beer or something. I don't even wait to hear an answer. I shut the door on my SUV and pull out of the guarded lot to head home.

It takes no time at all to get home, and I park in the garage and make my way into the house. I hate this feeling, but I don't know how to shake it. Something spectacular happened between Bear and me. Did he change his mind, though? Did Nash tell him it's his job or me, he had to choose?

Fuck, I didn't even think of that. I kick off my shoes and am about to fall on the couch when my doorbell rings.

I hold my breath as I practically run to look out

the peephole. It's him. It's Bear. I take a deep breath and let it out before pulling the door open. I do my best to keep my voice calm. "Hey."

He starts to walk in the door, and I put my hand to his chest to stop him. "Wait. You think you can ignore me, act like nothing happened and then what, you show up like I'm some dark secret you need to keep hidden from your buddies?"

His face is intense, and he looks furious. "No, I don't want to hide you. Every one of the guys knows how I feel about you."

I barely hold in my laugh. "Oh well, good, that's great. I'm glad they know how you feel, because I don't have a fuckin' clue."

His eyes go round, surprised by the curse word, I'm sure. I may work with a bunch of men, but I usually don't cuss. He grips the door. "Let me in, and I'll show you how I feel about you."

"No." I jut my chin at him. "Tell me."

"I love you, Sam. I have since the day you walked into the warehouse with Walker and I thought you were with him. He may have saved my life before, but I swear I was ready to kick his ass in that moment."

"There's nothing going on with Walker and me," I mutter to him in frustration. What is it with everyone thinking Walker and I had something going... And then it hits me. "Wait... did you just say you love me?"

He shrugs. "Yeah. I do too."

I almost reach for him, but I stop myself. "So what does that mean? We have to hide this or I'm out of a job? Is that why you ignored me? I saw you talking to Nash."

"Can we talk about this inside?"

I move to the side and wave him in. He walks in and looks around my small living room. "Have a seat."

He sits on the closest chair and pulls me down onto his lap.

I struggle to get up, but he keeps me in place. "I'll tell you everything, but I haven't had you in my arms in awhile, and I need this, Sam. Please give it to me."

When I agree, it seems his whole body relaxes underneath me, and his voice is soft and smooth as he starts to talk. "I talked to Nash and told him that I wasn't giving you up. Surprisingly, he's okay with it. We don't have to hide it, and he said that he needs us both, so you don't have to worry about your job or anything. But he did say that for a while, we will do separate missions."

I put my hand on his neck and force him to look at me. "That sounds reasonable. What's the problem?"

"I'll worry about you. How can I stay here and let you go into danger? I don't know if I can be that man or not."

I lean into him and bury my head in his neck. "I know, Bear. But I'll feel the same way when you have to leave."

He takes a deep breath. "And the reason I was so quiet afterwards—well, it's always hard afterwards for me. I wish I could say I never think about my past, but I do. Sometimes, I just need time by myself to work it out. I'm sorry if you thought I was trying to hide what I felt for you."

"I understand. But I want you to know I'm always here for you. I hate seeing you alone... you don't have to be. Even if you just want to sit next to me and hold my hand, I can do that and let you process it all. I just want to be there for you."

His eyes darken. "I'd like that."

I know he's really struggling with this. "Liam."

Surprised that I called him by name, he looks at me wide-eyed. I kiss his chin, his cheeks, and finally his lips. His arms tighten around me, and I could about get lost in the kiss, but before I do, I know I need to tell him. I pull away, gasping. "I love you, Liam James. I love you so much. I know this will be hard, but we'll figure it out. We'll make it work."

He rests his head against mine. "We'll have to, Sam. Because you're mine now."

"And you're mine," I tell him before leaning in and pressing my lips to his.

EPILOGUE

BEAR

"Another successful mission. I'm proud of all the hard work, everyone," Nash says in the front of the room.

It's the day after we got back, and thankfully it seems today is not going to be a long day. Nash confirms that when Colt asks, "What's next?"

Nash crosses his arms on his chest. "We have a few days. I have Dylan looking into a few things, but we'll be home for a few days at least."

"Yes!" Colt, Aiden, and John all say at the same time. It seems that everyone is tired and ready to rest up.

Knox keeps looking at his phone and seems preoccupied.

"All right, guys, I get it. Let's make it an early day. I'll keep in touch."

Everyone starts walking out of the office, and I watch as Sam gets to the door, turns, and smiles at me before walking out. We spent the night together last night, and if I have my choice, we will be doing the same from here on out.

Knox is walking, staring at a picture on his phone. "You okay, Knox?"

He startles as if he didn't notice me walking next to him. "Uh, yeah, a friend called in a favor. I'm heading to Knoxville."

"Anything I can help with?" I ask, because the look on his face tells me that it's not just a friendly favor.

"No. Well, I don't think so anyway."

I hit him on the back. "Call if you need anything."

He nods. "Thanks, Bear." And then walks off in the direction to Dylan's office.

I walk down the hallway, straight for Sam's office. I get inside and shut the door, and she's leaning on her desk as if she's been waiting on me.

I can't resist, and I walk straight to her and pull her into my arms for a kiss. We talked about boundaries last night, and it seems I'm already breaking one of the rules she made up of no making out in the office.

I force myself to pull away. "Sorry about that. You coming to my house tonight?"

"Sure." She shrugs and then holds her hand up. She starts taking the ring off her finger. "Here you go. I forgot to give you this back last night."

I grab on to her hands to stop her. "That's okay. Keep it on."

She stops and looks at me with her mouth wide open. "What do you mean keep it on?"

I show her my hand. "I'm still wearing mine."

She puts her hand on her hip. "I can't wear a ring you bought for someone else."

"I bought it the day I met you. And one day you're going to wear it for real. Until you're ready for that, you can wear it so people know you're taken."

She holds her hand up between us. "You bought this the day you met me. Like you bought it thinking I'd wear it one day?"

I thread our fingers together. "Fuck, I hoped so."

She swallows and bites her lip. "What if I want it to be real?"

My hands automatically tighten on her. "What are you saying?"

She shakes her head and smiles at me. Her big blue eyes are doing nothing to hide how she feels about me. It's as clear as the Whiskey Run sky at night. "I'm saying that if you asked me, I'd say yes."

I grab on to her tightly by the shoulders and then realize what I'm doing and gentle my hold. "Don't fuck with me, Sam."

She laughs. "I'm not."

I don't hesitate. I drop to a knee in front of her. "I love you, Sam. I want to spend the rest of my life loving you. Will you marry me?"

She has tears rolling down her cheeks. "Yes. I love you, Liam James."

I stand up and pick her up in one smooth motion. I swing her around and kiss her until she's breathless. The rule of no making out at the office will have to start tomorrow because there's no way I can stop now. She's mine now... forever.

GET KNOX's story in Whiskey Run: Heroes - Rescuing Karina

WHISKEY RUN SERIES

Want more of Whiskey Run?

Whiskey Run

Faithful - He's the hot, say-it-like-it-is cowboy, and he won't stop until he gets the woman he wants.

Captivated - She's a beautiful woman on the run... and I'm going to be the one to keep her.

Obsessed - She's loved him since high school and now he's back.

Seduced - He's a football player that falls in love with the small town girl.

Devoted - She's a plus size model and he's a small town mechanic.

Whiskey Run: Savage Ink

Virile - He won't let her go until he puts his mark on her.

Torrid - He'll do anything to give her what she wants.

Rigid - If you love reading about emotionally wounded men and the women that help them overcome their past, then you'll love Dawson and Emily's story.

Whiskey Run: Cowboys Love Curves

Obsessed Cowboy - She's the preacher's daughter and she's off limits.

Whiskey Run: Heroes

Ransom - He's on a mission he can't lose.

Redeem - He's in love with his sister's best friend.

Submit - She's his fake wife but he wants to make it real.

Rescuing Karina - An old threat sparks a new love

Forbid - They have a secret romance but he's about to stake his claim.

FREE BOOKS

Want FREE BOOKS?
Go to www.authorhopeford.com/freebies

JOIN ME!

JOIN MY NEWSLETTER & READERS
GROUP

www.AuthorHopeFord.com/Subscribe

JOIN MY READERS GROUP ON FACEBOOK

www.FB.com/groups/hopeford

Find Hope Ford at www.authorhopeford.com

ABOUT THE AUTHOR

USA Today Bestselling Author Hope Ford writes short, steamy, sweet romances. She loves tattooed, alpha men, instant love stories, and ALWAYS happily ever afters. She has over 100 books and they are all available on Amazon.

To find me on Pinterest, Instagram, Facebook, Goodreads, and more:

www.AuthorHopeFord.com/follow-me

Printed in Great Britain
by Amazon